This book belongs to

_____

Published by Scholastic Inc., 90 Old Sherman Turnpike, Danbury, Connecticut 06816.

ISBN: 0-7172-9956-2

Printed in the U.S.A.

First Scholastic printing, June 2006

LarryBoy AND THE GOLDEN GUM BALLS

A Lesson in Being Humble

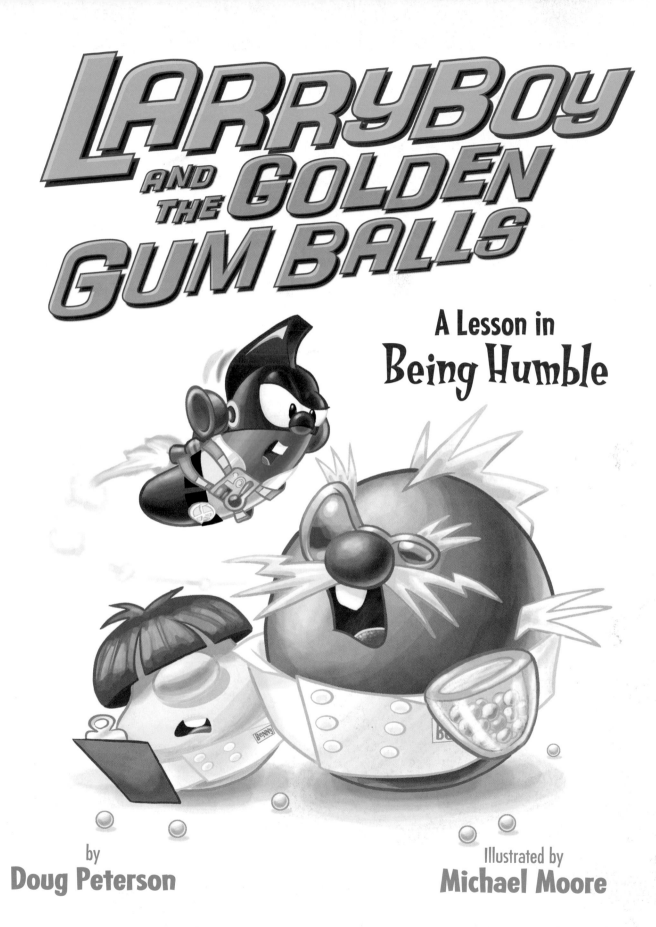

by
Doug Peterson

Illustrated by
Michael Moore

SCHOLASTIC INC.

New York Toronto London Auckland Sydney
Mexico City New Delhi Hong Kong Buenos Aires

Outside, a terrible thunderstorm raged. But inside Bubble-Gum Tower, excitement was in the air.

"Ladies and gentlemen, you are about to see the most amazing gum balls in the world!" said Dr. Bubba Gumm, world-famous scientist at the Bumblyburg Gum Company.

Dr. Gumm lifted the lid to reveal dozens of Golden Gum Balls. "I call it Bumble-Gum—the first gum that **never** loses its taste!" he said.

Everyone around the large table gasped.

Lightning **flashed**. Thunder **crashed**.

Larry the Cucumber just groaned. He had been playing with his gum and accidentally got it stuck to his nose.

"I invented this gum **all by myself**," boasted Bubba.

This time, Bubba's assistant gasped. Benny, the assistant, knew that his bragging boss had just lied. Bubba didn't invent Bumble-Gum—Benny did!

Lightning **flashed**. Thunder **crashed**.

Larry yelped. His nose had become stuck to the table with gum.

"I'll pass around the gum balls so you can try one yourselves," Bubba said. "This gum doesn't lose its taste—ever!"

But as Bubba picked up the bowl, a bolt of lightning suddenly sizzled across the sky, blasting the top floor of Bubble-Gum Tower.

Bubba lit up like a Christmas tree. Sparks flew! His hair shot up and stood on end. But what happened next was even more incredible.

Bubba turned bubble-gum pink and became very sticky—
and very stretchy. Somehow, lightning had caused all of the
powers of gum to jump from the gum balls into the scientist.
Lightning **flashed**. Thunder **crashed**.

Larry groaned. By this time, he had jerked his nose free
from the table. But as he did, he went flying. He was now
stuck, nose-first and upside down, against the wall.

Meanwhile, Bubba had gone completely bonkers. He grew bigger and bigger, like a monstrous bubble-gum bubble. "I am the greatest! And the Golden Gum Balls are mine!" Bubba boasted.

"But that isn't fair!" Benny yelled. "You didn't invent Bumble-Gum—I did!"

"Silence!" Bubba boomed. The mad scientist shot out a sticky arm of gum, like an octopus, and snagged Benny. Then he jammed Benny upside down into a trash can.

Meanwhile, Larry's faithful butler, Alfred, yanked him loose from the wall. "Master Larry, you've got to stop Dr. Bubba!" said Alfred. "He's filled with pride. He thinks he's better than everyone else. He's become . . . ," Alfred said, pausing dramatically. "He's become **stuck up!**"

"Help is on the way!" Larry shouted, with the wad of gum now stuck to his back. Larry leaped into a coat closet. A split second later he hopped back out, dressed as Bumblyburg's most fearless superhero—**LarryBoy!** He struck a heroic pose—with a coat hanger stuck to the gum on his back.

Bubba had grown as big as a bubble-gum car. "I am the smartest person alive!" he bellowed. Bursting through the outer wall, Bubba began to climb down the outside of the building. "Not so fast, sticky fingers," declared LarryBoy. "Being smarter doesn't make you better than everyone. You need to be humble. You need to think of others—not just yourself!"

LarryBoy put on the Larry-Jetpack so that he could
chase the monster. But there was one itsy-bitsy problem.
He put the jetpack on backward.
"Wait, LarryBoy!" shouted Alfred—too late.

LarryBoy pushed the Zoom
button, and the jetpack shot
him backward across the room.
Smack! He crashed
through the wall—and the next
wall and the wall after that.

THONK!

ZIP!

Bubba

Puffed up with pride, Bubba Gumm was now bigger than a bubble-gum bus. He headed for the Bubble-Gum Factory to steal all of the company's gum. "I am the biggest and strongest!" bragged Bubba.

"But being bigger doesn't make you better than everyone!" LarryBoy shouted, leaping into view. "Take this!" LarryBoy fired a plunger.

The plunger stuck to Bubba's gummy back. Then LarryBoy took off on his jetpack, hoping to drag Bubba away. But Bubba was too strong. He yanked LarryBoy across the parking lot.

"I just realized something," Alfred suddenly said
to LarryBoy, loud and clear over the Larry-Radio.
"Bubba thinks he's better than everyone
because he's smarter and bigger and
stronger. But he *isn't* the tallest."
"Come again?" asked LarryBoy.
"Look at the top of Bubble-
Gum Tower," said Alfred.

LarryBoy stared up at the pointy antenna sticking up from the 100th floor.

"Bubba is **not** as tall as that," Alfred said.

"Good point," said LarryBoy. "I think I know what you're getting at."

So the Purple Protector called out to the mad doctor. "Hey Bubba! You may be smarter and bigger than everyone. But you aren't the tallest!"

Bubba came to a sudden stop. "What are you talking about, PickleBoy?" Bubba yelled.

19

"You aren't the tallest," LarryBoy repeated. He motioned toward the tip-top of Bubble-Gum Tower. "That antenna is higher than you."

"We'll see about that," snarled Bubba, who was now as big as a bubble-gum boat. He climbed up and up and up. LarryBoy was dragged along.

Just past the 100th floor, the bubble-gum bad guy declared to all of Bumblyburg, "I am the smartest and biggest and strongest **and** the tallest!"

Then Bubba climbed to the very tip of the building's antenna. "And that makes me—!"

After Bubba plopped down on the pointy tip
of the antenna, he popped! His bubble-gum body
exploded and gum flew everywhere.

Instantly Bubba was back to normal—his small, ordinary self. There was only one teeny-weeny problem: he was falling.

Bubba tumbled from the top of Bubble-Gum Tower, dragging LarryBoy behind him.

"AAAHHHHHHHHH!"

Just before they smashed into the
ground, LarryBoy gained control of his
jetpack. Then he soared into the sky, saving
them both from a terrible fall.

The next day, Bubba was a new person. After the long fall, he realized he was no better than other people. No matter how smart or big or strong he was, God loved him just the same as everyone else—a lot!

Bubba even told everyone that Benny, his assistant, was the one who really invented Bumble-Gum.

"So today, let me show you Benny's greatest invention," Bubba announced. "But we're no longer calling it Bumble-Gum. It's now called Humble-Gum!"

Everyone cheered.

Everyone except for Larry, that is. His nose was stuck to the door—with gum, of course.

. . . If you are proud, you will fall.
Proverbs 16:18